Explorers Past and Present

Written by
Jill Atkins

Hundreds of years ago, there were no cars, bikes, buses, trains or planes, so most people didn't travel far.

But there were camels and donkeys and ships, so a few people started exploring the world.

Marco Polo was from Italy. He travelled to China along a trading path called **The Silk Road**.

He learnt about Chinese inventions such as paper money and gunpowder. No one in Italy had heard of such things!

A city on the Silk Road

People knew that the Earth was round. They thought that somewhere across the sea there could be another, quicker way to China.

Christopher Columbus thought he would try to find it. He left the coast of Spain with three sailing ships. It took many weeks to cross the Atlantic.

At last, they sighted land! They had arrived in **The Bahamas**, but Columbus thought he had reached China!

He was astonished at the rich forests and palm trees he found there. It was a different world!

Columbus made a total of four trips across the Atlantic.

At that time, nobody knew that some men from **Norway** had sailed across to America four hundred years ahead of them!

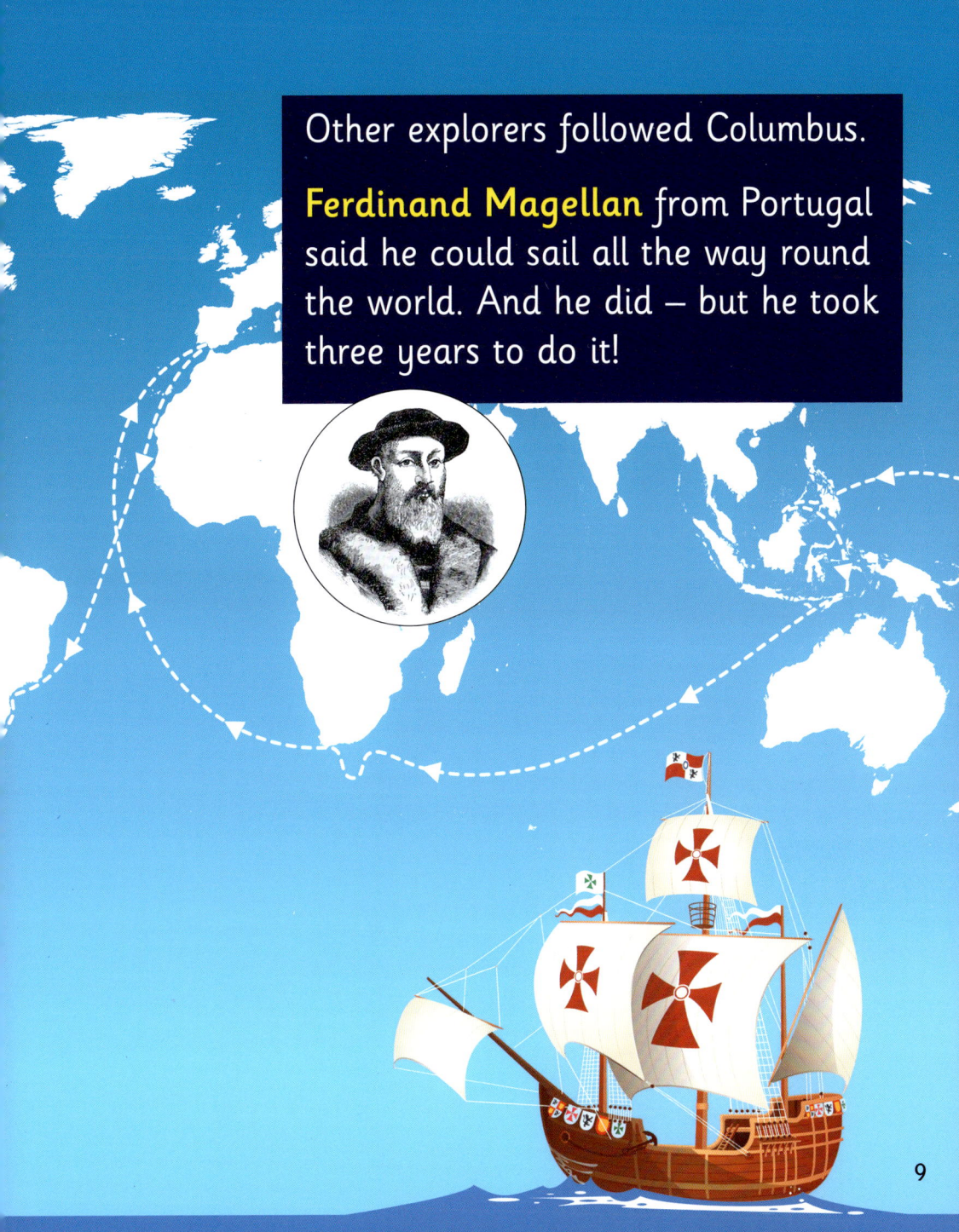

Other explorers followed Columbus.

Ferdinand Magellan from Portugal said he could sail all the way round the world. And he did – but he took three years to do it!

Scott's team at the South Pole

A hundred years ago, the British man **Robert Scott** and the explorer **Amundsen**, from Norway, raced each other to be the first to reach the South Pole.

When Scott finally got to the South Pole, he found that Amundsen had beaten him to it!

In the past, most explorers were men, but not all!

Way ahead of Columbus, an Icelandic lady called **Gudrid** travelled from Iceland to Greenland and then on to North America.

Mary Seacole, from Jamaica, travelled far and wide to care for sick people.

Nellie Bly, from America, went round the world in just over seventy days, travelling by train, steamship, horse, donkey and rickshaw. She took just one small bag and one dress!

Now there are many female explorers.

Erika Bergman, from Germany, is a deep-sea robot pilot. She explores the icy waters of the Arctic.

Ellen MacArthur set a world record for sailing around the world, non-stop and on her own.

People have been exploring the Earth for hundreds of years, but now exploration goes much further.

Men have landed on the Moon.

Male and female astronauts from many nations stay and work on space stations. What will they discover?

Now, rovers like this one are exploring the planet Mars.

Anyone can be an explorer. You can visit caves, mountains or tropical forests.

Would you like to be an explorer? Where would you like to go?